About Leaf Books

Our mission is to provide readers with a pocket-sized read in the places where they are waiting, relaxing, taking a break. We aim to support writers by giving them a new market for their short stories and short non-fiction.

Don't forget to visit our website www.leafbooks.co.uk to tell us what you think of this book and to learn more about the writer and our other services.

Enjoy!

First published by Leaf Books Ltd in 2006
Copyright © Jackie Spry

Cover illustration © David Fisher

Leaf Books are proud to be working with
The University of Glamorgan

www.leafbooks.co.uk

Leaf
GTi Suite,
Valleys Innovation Centre,
Navigation Park,
Abercynon,
CF45 4SN

Printed by Allprint
www.allprint.ltd.uk

ISBN 1-905599-14-5
ISBN 978-1-905599-14-1

Dead Man's Bells

by

Jackie Spry

Jackie Spry is a musician who began writing as a means of relaxation from demanding semiquavers. Story writing at the computer keyboard proved just as addictive as sonata playing on the piano's ivories. Jackie has had many short stories published in magazines. In 2004 she was the winner of BBC Radio Stoke's short story competition. She is a part time music lecturer at the University of Salford. Jackie lives in Staffordshire with her husband, Bill, and is a member of Congleton Writers' Forum.

Dead Man's Bells

They were late. David frowned into the mirror and let the weight of his right foot collapse onto the accelerator. A froth of cow parsley assailed both sides of the old Vauxhall and hawthorn spines scratched at the windows as they hurtled down past Benson's Farm.

'Stop the car!' Shirley called.

'What on earth for? We're already going to be unpopular with Gina.'

'I've seen something.'

David braked, reversed a few yards and pulled the car into an opening by a five–barred gate.

Shirley got out of the car and opened the boot. Stacks of old newspapers intended for the recycling container had veered into carrier bags of old yoghurt pots and plastic lemonade bottles. She rummaged through black bin liners and pulled out a large, empty margarine tub. She picked up a white fork, still sticky from Monday's snack lunch, and started to climb the steep bank.

David turned off the ignition and sighed. He watched his wife in her grey dress grappling with the brambles until she reached the tall, pink spikes. She bent down and started to dig carefully around one plant. If she pushed too hard the fork would snap. Gently she levered the foxglove with its soft, wide leaves out of its nest. The soil was still damp and clung to the strings of the roots. Shirley stuffed the clump into the tub and smoothed the surface. Cradling the plant in the crook of her left arm, she slithered down the bank. Her heels ripped into the cushion of moss that lined the lower edge.

She threw the fork back into the boot of the car and took out an old pair of sandals. At least they were clean. Shirley changed out of her black patent shoes and brushed her dress with the back of her fingers. She would have to wash her hands properly at Gina's.

She sat back in the car with her booty.

'Digitalis,' said David. 'It's poisonous.'

'I know,' said Shirley, smiling to herself,

'but it's pretty, and we can't go empty handed, can we?'

David started the car and they set off up the hill. He wondered if he might be able to persuade Shirley to see Doctor Sanderson.

Shirley turned and studied her husband's profile. Beneath the thin layers of silver hair and pink skin she could see into the snakes and ladders of his mind. She traced the falling curve of their dull fortnight in Bournemouth: David striding ahead of her on the beach, David listening to Radio Three in the evenings. She charted the peaking line of elation leading to the meal ahead. Three, maybe four, hours with Gina, even if it was in the quaint decorum of his wife's company.

They turned the last corner and Leydens Cottage appeared before them, its honeyed walls beckoning seductively.

'Gina's done wonders with the place,' said David.

'She can afford it.' Shirley wedged the margarine tub more tightly between her feet. The downy undersides of the foxglove leaves felt comforting on her calves.

Leydens was not the sort of house that had attracted much interest from local buyers when it came on the market two years ago. It had been empty for too long. The gutters leaked. The window frames were rotten. The pointing needed serious attention. Inside the flock wallpaper drooped.

But Gina Harte had vision. Now that she was comfortably divorced, she was looking for a little nook of rural England where she could live happily ever after. Gina Harte had money. She bought Leydens and employed builders to restore the cottage to a cut above its former glory. The stone was cleaned, new windows sparkled, the oak floors shone and Gina moved in.

'Sorry we're late,' said David. 'Shirley couldn't find her handbag.'

'That's all right. Come in, come in!'

Gina embraced her guests and Shirley felt the brush of pearly coral masking thin lips. There was something ludicrous about a kiss from her husband's mistress.

'I've missed you both so much,' said Gina.

Liar, thought Shirley. Gina had missed David.

'We've only been away for two weeks,' said Shirley.

'I know, but it seems like ages and I can't wait to hear all about Bournemouth.'

David and Shirley followed Gina's swaying floral caftan down the polished corridor to the long room at the back. Sunshine had disappeared from this side of the house, but the silky glow of table lamps shone onto the terracotta tiles and Turkish rugs. Candles flickering with the scent of vanilla had been placed on the oak dresser. At the end of the room stood a grand piano, waiting, like a sleek black panther, to spring into action. A round table, covered with a cream linen cloth, had been laid for three.

Shirley blinked. She was unaccustomed to such style and comfort. Then she realised she was still clutching the foxglove.

'This is for you,' said Shirley, handing Gina her gift, in a moment of modest triumph.

'How perfectly lovely! How very English! Thank you.'

Shirley went to the bathroom and washed her hands. When she returned, there was no sign of the plant. Perhaps Gina had confined it to the bin.

'Will you have a glass of wine with me, Shirley?' asked Gina. 'I'm just fixing David his usual.'

'That would be nice.'

Shirley watched as Gina mixed the whisky and dry ginger, the shades of amber swirling easily together. Shirley had been married to David for forty-two years but even now she didn't know the correct proportions of David's *usual*. Her husband always poured his own drinks at home.

'So, what did you get up to? Where did you stay?' The golden hoops of Gina's earrings bobbed excitedly.

'At the Fairview,' said David.

'I don't think I know it.'

'It's a guesthouse,' said Shirley. She noticed her husband wince at the word, which, six months ago, he would have been quite happy to use himself. 'Homely, and very reasonable with the evening meal.'

'Sounds sweet. When Fred was alive we used to go to The Marine Gardens. A whole crowd of us went down there for the Easter Bank Holiday. It was all such fun, partying until the early hours. Did I tell you about the time Nobby died on us? Dear old Nobby. One day, it must have been about half past eleven in the morning, and nobody had seen him. So Fred went up and knocked on his bedroom door. No reply. Fred got one of the maids to unlock the door. It was a bit of a shock when they found poor Nobby dead as a dodo. And I don't mean dead tucked up in bed, but sprawled out on the sheet, with not a stitch on. Next to his body was a pair of pink suspenders and a little note thanking him for a wonderful time. There was a terrible fuss because, at first, they thought it was murder. But it turned out that Nobby had had a massive heart attack. What a way to go!'

David let out a guffaw. It took Shirley by

surprise: she had forgotten the sound of her husband's laughter.

'Be a darling, David, and pour us all some of this red wine. I've done a beef chilli.' Gina went into the kitchen and began to take dishes out of the oven.

She leaned round the doorway and said, 'Mind you, they never did find out who was with Nobby that night.'

'Took his secret to the grave with him, I suppose.' David twirled the stem of his glass slowly.

'A wise move,' remarked Shirley. 'It's always best to keep an affair secret, especially when it's close to home.'

David stared at his wife. He would ring Doctor Sanderson tomorrow and make an appointment for Shirley.

'Nothing wise about dying,' he said. 'Well, not on such a beautiful evening as this.'

Gina brought in a tomato salsa, brown rice and a large dish of chilli.

'Help yourselves!'

By way of encouragement Gina put her right

hand onto David's shoulder, where she left it resting for just a moment too long. Shirley wouldn't make a scene. It wasn't her style.

Shirley had first met Gina in Jackson's.

'Don't they do organic?' she'd asked Shirley.

'You'll have to go into Bury for that. It's a bit limited here.'

'Never mind. I can make do. It's only for me, after all.' She fingered the dry, rubbery bloom of the broccoli. 'I've just moved in on the other side of Marfield.'

Shirley didn't normally strike up a conversation with somebody she didn't know. But it made her feel slightly important to be able to answer Gina's enquiries. Did the chemist's shut during the lunch hour? Which was the most reliable taxi service to the station? How often did the trains run on the London line? If Shirley had been new to a place she would have found out all this information by asking the relevant authorities or collecting train timetables. After all, how could you rely on somebody you'd just met in the greengrocer's? But Gina was different. She liked to chat.

In an uncharacteristic gesture of welcome, Shirley invited Gina round for a coffee at Albert Street the next morning.

And so there had begun an unequal alliance, where Shirley had perched on the empty pan of the scales, tipped up by the weight of Gina's exuberance. Two passionate but tempestuous marriages had somehow left Gina with an increased vigour for life. There had been no children. There would have been no room.

Gina had travelled. She brought photos for Shirley's inspection; Gina and Fred dancing along behind a New Orleans jazz band at the Mardi Gras; Gina and Johnny, twined together on a sunbed by the pool of a Tuscan villa.

'Won't you find it rather quiet in Marfield?' Shirley had asked. 'Nothing ever happens here.'

'I don't believe it. Isn't there a local drama group or an art society?'

'There's David's choir.'

'A choir? How wonderful!'

'They meet on Wednesday evenings. David's a retired piano teacher. Well, not really retired, he still has a few pupils.'

'I had lessons when I was younger. I still play a bit. I'd love to take it up again, properly, I mean.'

Gina needed no encouragement.

'Teach me, teach me, please, David!' she'd pleaded the first time she'd met David in the dull, brown sitting room at Albert Street.

'Well, I don't know.' David had seemed reluctant at first, nervous even. 'I don't really want to take on any more pupils.'

'I promise I'll do my practice and Grandma Arnold's piano is just lying there, waiting to be brought to life again. It seems such a waste of a Steinway. I didn't think I'd be able to have it at the cottage, but once that wall was down and I opened up the room, I knew the piano would fit in perfectly.'

'A Steinway, you say? You didn't tell me your friend had a piano,' David looked accusingly at Shirley.

'I forgot.'

'It's a Steinway grand,' Gina was saying.

'I wouldn't mind a play on that.' David wasn't nervous anymore.

'Come round, David. Anytime you like.'

A week later Gina began her Thursday afternoon piano lessons with David.

'I'll just do it for a few weeks,' he'd said. 'She won't want to stick at it, but it'll give me a chance to play on a decent piano.'

The upright in the corner at Albert Street had seen better days. There had been too many ham–fisted pupils, most of whom would rather have been emulating Beckham than Beethoven. David couldn't afford to buy a new instrument. Piano teaching didn't pay well. There was a time when David had thought he might make it as a soloist, but that was long ago. He didn't even enjoy teaching, apart from the occasional gifted young pupil, who would leave him after a couple of years and move on to Chetham's School of Music.

Shirley, too, thought Gina's lessons wouldn't last for long. Her husband didn't like women who talked too much. The whole thing was nothing more than an excuse for David to play on the Steinway. Besides, Gina wouldn't tolerate the regime of scales and arpeggios that David liked to inflict on his pupils.

But after three or four weeks Shirley knew that the Thursday piano lessons weren't going to finish. David's voice had a new note of eagerness, excitement even, when he returned from Leydens Cottage.

'Gina's actually quite good. She played me a Brahms Intermezzo this afternoon, the one in E flat. It's a long time since I heard anybody play it so musically. Of course, she's a bit rusty, but we can work on that.'

Gina began to practise again. Her playing flourished, along with David's teaching. The Thursday afternoon lessons grew longer and David wouldn't get back to Albert Street until late in the evening.

Shirley had never really understood David's world of music. She would dutifully go to all of his choir concerts, serving tea and biscuits in the intervals, but she was not a part of the music. All those black lines and squiggles, crowding like little aliens onto the white page. Shirley preferred her cross stitch. With each stab of the needle you could build up a reliable pattern of colours that would grow into a crinolined lady or a narrow boat on a Midlands canal.

She was quite happy to sit sewing in the kitchen, when John and Bea came round on Sundays to play piano trios with David. And when her eyes tired of cross stitching she could always ring her daughter in Milton Keynes, although these days Amanda never seemed to be at home.

Shirley's heydays had been Amanda's schooldays: cheering her daughter on Sports' Day, sewing on name tapes, organising tea parties for school friends. It had been a busy time, but David had kept his distance. He had his Bach Preludes and Fugues, his Mozart Sonatas. Amanda had shown no interest in her father's attempts to teach her the piano. Shirley never knew if David was disappointed. He didn't say anything. There was no point in discussing such matters.

18

Shirley could cope with John and Bea. She could cope with the members of David's choir. She had known them all for years. But Gina was different. Gina had no business popping up in their lives like this.

'This is tasty, Gina,' said David.

'I'm glad you like it. Of course, I had to go in to Sainsbury's. You can't get a decent piece of meat in Marfield, not to mention fresh coriander and limes.'

Shirley wondered why Gina had come to live in an English village, when her shopping list seemed more suited to one of those sultry South American countries. Shirley bought plain food. David always said he didn't like herbs and spices. But Shirley had discovered that her husband's tastes were changing.

'How's the phone box coming on, Shirley?' Gina was asking.

Shirley was currently cross stitching a red telephone box, such as you could only find used as a garden ornament or shower these days.

'It's nearly finished,' said Shirley.

'She's just got to add the torn up telephone directories and the yobbos pissing on the floor,' laughed David.

Shirley stared ahead.

'Take no notice of him!' said Gina. 'David, that was just a bit nasty.'

'Sorry,' he said.

Shirley couldn't remember the last time David had apologised.

'I'll help you clear this lot,' said David. He got up and, together, he and Gina took the empty plates into the kitchen. Shirley poured herself more wine. She heard the clatter of dishes over the buzz of their conversation.

When David returned to the table, Shirley thought she noticed a smudge of pearly coral on his shirt.

'What shall I open now, Gina? Red or white?' he asked. Gina came to the table with a blackcurrant cheesecake.

'Let's ask Shirley what she would like,' said Gina.

Shirley considered the matter. She knew

what she would like but the time wasn't yet quite right for telling.

'I don't mind,' she said.

Shirley bit into the cheesecake. She felt the berries smarting on her tongue. Gina and David were talking of Opus numbers and semiquavers, of Chopin Studies and Ravel's Sonatine. She drank more wine and pushed the remaining cheesecake to one side.

'It's a bit tart, isn't it?' said Gina.

David thought this amusing and sniggered. He must be drunk. Shirley began to wonder how they would get home.

'Why don't you both stay over?' Gina was saying. 'The bed's made up in the spare room.'

'Good idea,' said David. 'I don't think I ought to be driving.'

Shirley said nothing. She wanted to get back to Albert Street. She couldn't spend a night in Gina's house. The idea was preposterous.

'Why don't I make us some coffee?' she volunteered. 'You could play us one of your pieces, Gina. David's always telling me how well you're doing.'

She could tell that they were both surprised at the interest she had suddenly shown in Gina's progress. David looked pleased and Gina was already moving towards the piano.

'Well, that's very nice of you, Shirley. I've been practising the Prokofiev duet whilst you were away.'

'You mean the arrangement of the Romeo and Juliet Suite? Wonderful!' David jumped up. They jostled together, squeezing onto the single piano stool, laughing like school children. Shirley saw David's bulge of fat cushioning into Gina's ample hips, ageing flesh pressed together, stubby white finger nails brushing the plum glossed manicure, a streaky blonde hair falling onto David's shoulder. Was this how it had all started? She shivered and went out to the kitchen.

By the washing machine stood her foxglove, still stately, the leaves hardly wilting. Two hooded flowers had slipped the anchor of their stamens and fallen onto the floor.

Shirley opened the back door and stepped

outside. She breathed in the mustard scent of nasturtiums. From the long room she could hear Gina and David at the piano. The Montagues and Capulets were beginning to fight and a sudden blow of sharp discords helped to clear Shirley's mind from the effects of too much wine. New strands of thought were emerging inside her head. Orderly strands, not unlike her cross stitch patterns. They wouldn't let her down.

Shirley reached into her handbag and took out David's mobile phone. It was the phone that had made her late this evening. She'd had to search for it, before they'd left Albert Street. Shirley had known then that it might offer her escape. With darting movements she tapped the numbers into the black plastic of her lifeline. The taxi would be at Leydens in half an hour. Time to drink coffee together, politely, amiably even.

Shirley filled the kettle and switched it on. She set out three cups and saucers and marked two of them with spoons. She couldn't afford to make a mistake.

She picked up the two foxglove flowers and laid them carefully on a chopping board. The rhythm of clashing swords, strident and threatening, flew from the Steinway into the kitchen. Shirley sliced into the flowers' white necks, piercing their mottled throats. She struck at the pink, the mauve, the purple. She cut deep into the last forty years of silences and unuttered recriminations. She slashed at Gina's pearly coral lips and her plum glossed nails. The relentless pounding on the piano drove her onwards, as she hacked the limp foxglove bells into tiny pieces, the knife scoring criss-cross into the wood below. David and Gina were surging into the final thrust. Shirley raised her knife and echoed the fatal stab.

Mercutio was dead. The feuding families laid down their swords and Shirley put down her knife. Quietly, she divided the shredded petals into two. She scraped one small pile into David's cup, the other into Gina's. She covered the poison with coffee granules and added hot water and milk. In one cup a valiant fleck of purple still floated on the surface. With the back of a teaspoon, Shirley pushed it under the brown liquid. Then she made her own cup of coffee.

In the middle of the chopping board was a purplish blotch. It reminded Shirley of the birthmark on David's neck. She ran hot water and scrubbed unsuccessfully at the board with washing up liquid and an old brush. What did it matter? Gina wouldn't be here to see the stain.

Shirley took the small tray of cups into the long room. Then she fetched the foxglove plant and placed it in the middle of the table, where it graced the cream cloth with a kind of menacing beauty.

Gina and David had moved onto another movement. Their heads were bowed, almost in reverence, as they felt their way into Prokofiev's solemn harmonies. Shirley watched, waiting, listening. She saw Romeo standing at Juliet's tomb. Tonight, for the first and last time, music had touched Shirley's soul.

The pianists paused on the last chord. A curious tenderness came briefly over David's face before he spoke.

'Magnificent, Gina!' He put his arm around her. 'You must have put in a lot of practice.'

'It went well, didn't it?' Gina stood up and noticed Shirley sitting at the table. 'Did you enjoy our duet?'

'It had a kind of peculiar power,' said Shirley slowly. 'Your coffee's ready.'

'What's *that* thing doing there?' asked David, pointing at the foxglove. 'You can't put it on the table.' He picked up the plant and moved it onto the windowsill.

'I suppose you're right,' conceded Shirley. 'We can't have the flowers dropping into our coffee, can we? Dead Man's Bells we used to call them at school.'

Gina giggled, spluttering on her coffee. 'I thought for a moment you said Dead Man's Balls, Shirley.' She began to laugh wildly, rocking back on her chair, the gold hooped earrings swinging to and fro.

But this time David ignored Gina's joke. He wasn't listening to her.

'Dead Man's Bells, you said, Shirley?

26

You've got it wrong. The poison lies in the seeds and the leaves, not in the flowers.'

Shirley looked down, avoiding the eyes that tried to hook onto hers.

His voice crept along on the bottom line of its stave. 'You've got it all wrong. Can't you see, you've got everything wrong?'

Gina's chair was bolt upright and the gold hoops were still.

'What are you talking about, David?' she asked.

David didn't respond. He drank his coffee. Nobody spoke. Shirley wondered if David was right about the poison. She wondered if he was right about everything else. She didn't really care anymore. Her cold anger had drifted back to its own tomb, where, not quite sealed, it would remain.

The sound of the doorbell snapped into the silence.

'Who can that be at this time?' Gina asked.

'It's the taxi. I ordered it while you two were playing Romeo and Juliet.' She centred her cup neatly in the middle of its saucer. Without hurrying, she wiped her mouth on the crumpled serviette.

'Are you coming, David?'

OUT OF LOVE
Poetry Anthology

'Upset? Not even close, but I'm over him.'

For Valentine's Day, Leafran the 'In Love' and 'Out of Love' poetry competition. The response was spectacular.

The 'Out of Love' selection represents the best and bitterest of the entries received.

For more information about Leaf Books and our services, please visit our website:

www.leafbooks.co.uk

- Complete List of Leaf Books
- Writers' Biographies
- Readers' Forum
- Ebooks
- Audio Books
- MP3 Downloadable Books
- Stockists
- How to Submit a Story to Leaf
- Competitions
- Writers' Services
- Jobs with Leaf

Competitions and Submissions

The Leaf competition and submission calendar enables us to gather stories, non-fiction, poetry written by new and established writers in the UK and abroad.

Every entry or submission is read by at least two members of our readers' panel. The panel consists of book and story lovers who represent a wide selection of backgrounds and tastes. We are very proud of this selection procedure and believe it gives a fair chance to every writer who sends us their work.

Leaf Competitions Entry Form

Name_____

Address_____

_____

_____

Email _____

Phone_____

Competition Title _____

See Website for details of Competitions and closing dates.   www.leafbooks.co.uk

Title of Story/Piece/Poem

1._____

2._____

3._____

4._____

I enclose cheque, made payable to Leaf, for £_____ (£5.00 for each story, £2.50 for each poem, and £10 for each critique).

Please send entries to:

Leaf, Gti Suite, Valleys Innovation Centre Abercynon, CF45 4SN.